W9-AVF-961

Thanks to my parents and my ancestors
and all the folks from Oakey Streak!
—*D. P. W.*

For the good times we shared at our family reunions,
for my cousin Sandra Rochelle
—*D. J.*

Atheneum Books for Young Readers
An imprint of Simon & Schuster Children's Publishing Division
1230 Avenue of the Americas
New York, New York 10020
Text copyright © 1996 by Dee Parmer Woodtor
Illustrations copyright © 1996 by Dolores Johnson
All rights reserved including the right of reproduction in whole or in part in any form.
Book design by Angela Carlino
The text of this book is set in Fairfield.
The illustrations are etchings and aquatints with watercolor and colored pencils.
First edition
Printed in the United States of America
10   9   8   7   6   5   4   3   2   1
Library of Congress Cataloging-in-Publication Data
Woodtor, Dee.
Big meeting / by Dee Parmer Woodtor; illustrated by Dolores Johnson.—1st ed.
p.   cm.
Summary: Family from all over travel to the South to attend "Big Meeting" at the Bethel A.M.E. Church, where
they worship and get together to eat and renew old ties.
ISBN 0-689-31933-9
[1. Afro-Americans—Fiction. 2. Religious gatherings—Fiction. 3. Summer—Fiction. 4. Southern States—Fiction.]
I. Johnson, Dolores, ill. II. Title.
Pz7.W869Bi   1996
[Fic]—dc20   95-15299

Big Meeting

by Dee Parmer Woodtor
illustrated by Dolores Johnson

ATHENEUM BOOKS FOR YOUNG READERS

◄O►

Big Meeting! It happens the third week in August, in some places the second, when people get together Down Home. Down Home is where the dirt is red, the sky is blue, and berries and wild grapes are just waiting on you.

◄O►

◄○►

Heading Down Home, cars make a line on Interstate 65. They
will come from New York, Los Angeles, Detroit, Pittsburgh, Chicago,
and places in between. Some people even come by train—the
Hummingbird, City of New Orleans, the New York Central, the Panama
Limited. Aunt Nettie, Aunt Hazel, Uncle John, Aunt Bobbie, Con'
Henry, Con' Addie, Grandpa Ezra, Precious Jewel, Bubba—they all head
Down Home for this Big Meeting.

◄○►

‑‑◄○►‑

Down Home for us is Oakey Streak—out in the middle of nowhere
it seems. Off Highway 23, across the wooden bridge at Pigeon Creek,
under the trees that meet and bend to sweep our car and greet us with
a bouquet of twining vines, up another dusty road until, at last, we
see in the clearing a white house with a porch. Ol' Man Quessie
and his wife Bessie sit on their front porch, waiting.

The real greetings start right here when Grandma Bessie says,
"Y'all come on in, and stay awhile." And that is just what I am ready to
do! We get out of our cars and shake off all the dust. Right away, we
kick off our shoes. Down Home is a place to run free.

‑‑◄○►‑

On Saturday, the day before Big Meeting, Grandma Bessie and all of my aunts will cook all night while Grandpa Quessie rocks on the porch and tells stories to scare us. We go to sleep with our eyes open and watch for shadows from the blue moon on our stark white sheets. We sleep a dream-filled sleep.

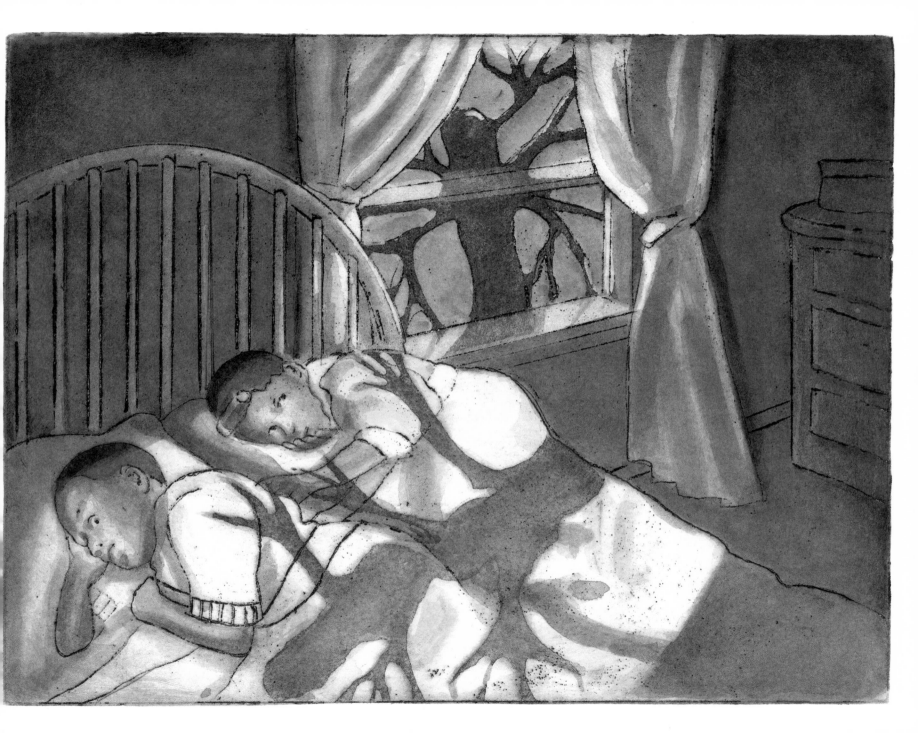

When we wake, we dress up in our best clothes, tie ribbons, wear bow ties and shoes that pinch our feet. We fidget and fuss until we look our best. Big Meeting has been tradition for so long, says Grandpa Quessie, he feels blessed that he hasn't missed a one.

At Little Bethel A.M.E. church the old oak tree shades some of the cars, and those who still ride wagons circle the yard. We hardly have had time to play when we are hushed and hurried inside.

We walk down the aisle of Bethel A.M.E. and sit in the front where all the children must. Aunt Hester sits behind us—she's in charge. In the Amen Corner, the deacons and deaconesses quietly sit, their hands folded. If we should start giggling at Ol' Man Kinzie who always prays too long, Aunt Hester will give us a good eyeball beating and a tap on the head with her fan. Big Meeting is serious business.

But our stomachs growl and our giggles almost escape. Heads bowed, our shoulders laugh instead, until we feel Aunt Hester's tapping fan. So we sit in the heat, listen to the fans beat against the ladies' bosoms. Their feet pat against the wooden floor. We watch the ushers, dressed in starchy white, guide visitors on tip-toe down the aisle. We stare at all the people—people from near and far—and wonder if Little Bethel will burst its seams. Aunt Hester rolls her eyes and nods. We turn our heads to the front.

"Listen," she says.

A hush spreads over Bethel A.M.E. as a tall man rises. He raises his hands as if they hold magic. His gaze moves from one side of the church to the other, and the arms of his robe sweep open like the wings of a bird. Reverend Lomax begins to speak.

"Yes, yes. We've all come to this Big Meeting like we've done before. Even the little children come—blessed are our children. We come year in, year out, from far and near. My friends, the time will come when we will meet no more." Then his voice rises. "But in the by and by we will meet again—yes, at the Biggest Meeting between long-ago family and friends. Our hearts pour out to those who've come and gone."

Everyone in Bethel A.M.E. cries out, "Yes! Yes! Amen." Reverend

Lomax stops and turns. Suddenly the sounds of a piano roar over our

heads followed by those of a bass guitar. We sit straight and wide-eyed.

We watch as the choir members open their mouths in wide O's.

The church begins to rock, the preacher begins to sway, feet begin to

beat, arms begin to fly. The ushers stand watch stiffly, their fans in

their hands. We rise from our seats and feel bathed in sound and

rhythm and words that we don't know but are sure we understand

until the preacher waves his hands for silence.

—◄O►—

One voice continues. Who can that be? Fearfully we turn our eyes to see Grandpa Quessie swaying from side to side, his hands on his seat, his head thrown back as he sings, "Ahhh-h Maaaa Zinnnng Graaaace" . . . and everyone joins in as he sings a song we've heard so many times before. Quietly, we wonder why these old people love sadness so.

But the sadness doesn't last. There is joy when the visitors are called on to testify—to tell how far they've come just to get home. Some shout, " 'Twas grace alone." But most say smaller things. And everybody talks some more, down the aisle, through the church door, out into the shade of the old oak tree.

—◄O►—

We stand on the church steps and watch the yard fill with hats and hugs and smiles. A hundred hands hold fans and handkerchiefs and then each other. We count to see how many hugs Aunt Hester gets from the big lady in the big hat who says, "Well, my goodness, good gracious alive, is that you?" One man has a wooden leg; there's a lady with skin as red as the dirt. There's another with moles, and a pretty girl with bluish skin and a gap in her front teeth. These people, they say, are our people, too.

Before long the food is ready for us all. I have some of Ms. Esther's dressing, June Bug has some chicken, Tiny has a big plate of dumplings, and Bubba eats too much. We bump into Aunt Hester and try to run away.

"Here's Jurleen's baby girl and boy. You remember Jurleen, don't you, Miss Minnie." Miss Minnie's long withered arm reaches out as she peeks from under her hat.

"Why, Jurleen has done just fine. What's your name, baby?" I laugh and roll my eyes and look away. "My name is Ethelene, but I like being called Sweet Pea. And this is Bubba, but his real name is James."

Before Aunt Hester can say, "Now meet your Con' Sukey and Uncle Joe," we slip away—off down the road where the courting people meet.

—◀○▶—

We kick our socks and shoes from our feet and run from Uncle Jim,
who shouts that we're in more trouble than we know, 'cause Aunt
Hester didn't tell us that we could go. We run away again taking the
shortcut through the old meeting hall, out the back door, and suddenly,
names jump out at us from the tall white headstones reaching from the
red dirt into a blue sky—Samuel C. and Mattie Brewer, Dilsey Jones,
Infant Wendell Mathelsa and Sula Kinzie. We know some of these
names. Uncle Jim catches up and tells us these people are also
our people. "They always come to Big Meeting, too."

—◀○▶—

—◄O►—

As we walk back, tarrying behind, we feel awful small. We make
patterns in the sand with our still bare feet and sing quiet rhyming
chants. Aunt Hester stands looking at us with her hand on her hip.
But she says she's too tired to do anything anymore. But just wait till
we get . . . the minute we reach Quessie's porch, she will . . . and
how could we miss all this food—Aunt Bobbie's dumplings, Ms. Sula's
caramel cake. . . . Little does she know that we've made all
the rounds. We took care of our business, too.

—◄O►—

—◄O►—

The sun is almost the last to leave Bethel A.M.E. We ride away

with the windows open to cool piney breezes rising from the woods.

When we reach the yard, we jump down for one last game before the

moon rises behind the house. We still have one more week Down Home

before it's time to go "Up South" as Ol' Man Quessie says. A week to

eat red-ripe tomatoes off the vine, to catch minnows in the stream.

—◄O►—

A week to spend time with more of our people, before our car slowly drives away, over the bridge at Pigeon Creek, beneath the trees that meet and bow and sag and say good-bye.